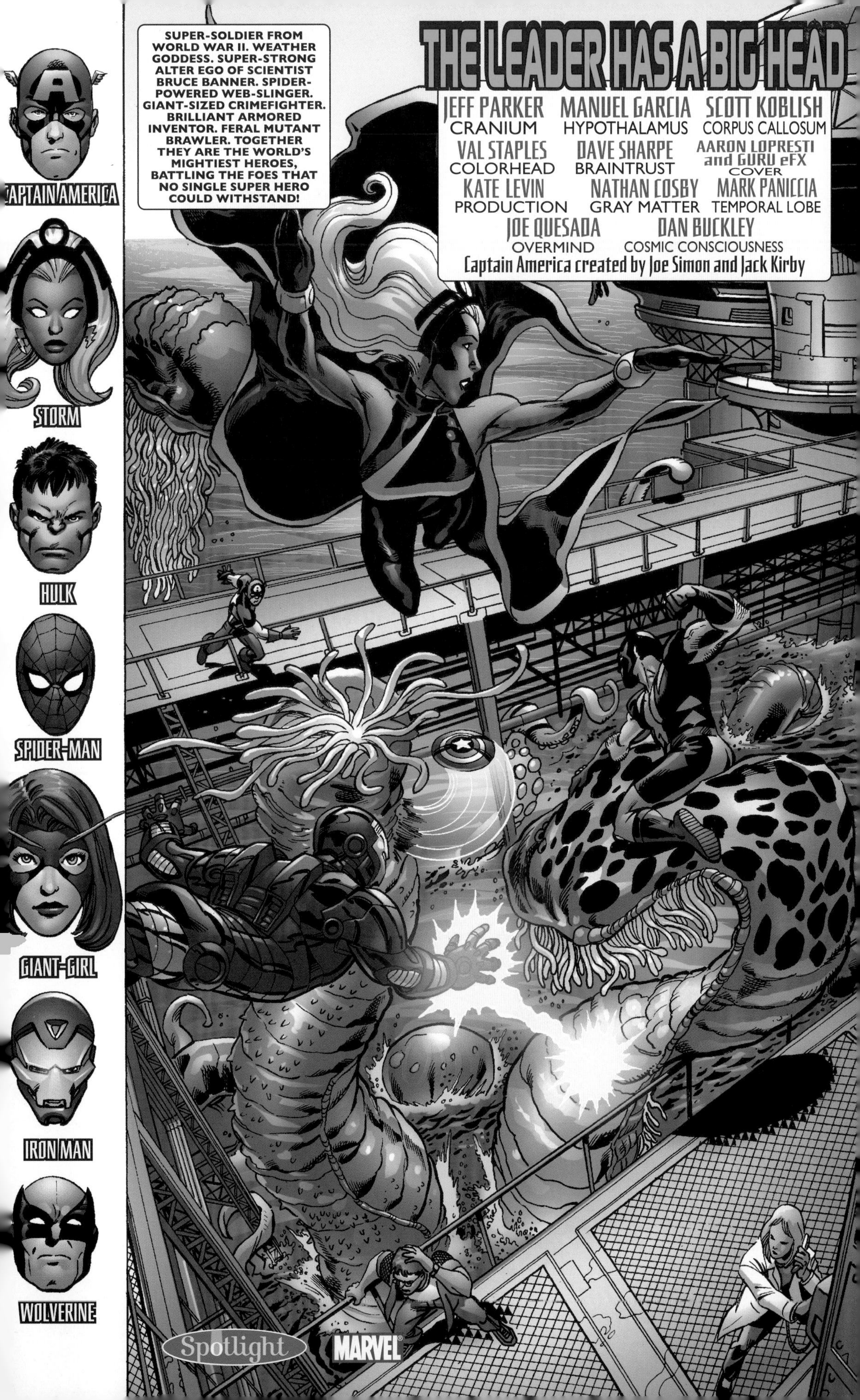
CAPTAIN AMERICA
STORM
HULK
SPIDER-MAN
GIANT-GIRL
IRON MAN
WOLVERINE
SUPER-SOLDIER FROM WORLD WAR II. WEATHER GODDESS. SUPER-STRONG ALTER EGO OF SCIENTIST BRUCE BANNER. SPIDER-POWERED WEB-SLINGER. GIANT-SIZED CRIMEFIGHTER. BRILLIANT ARMORED INVENTOR. FERAL MUTANT BRAWLER. TOGETHER THEY ARE THE WORLD'S MIGHTIEST HEROES, BATTLING THE FOES THAT NO SINGLE SUPER HERO COULD WITHSTAND!
THE LEADER HAS A BIG HEAD
JEFF PARKER CRANIUM
MANUEL GARCIA HYPOTHALAMUS
SCOTT KOBLISH CORPUS CALLOSUM
VAL STAPLES COLORHEAD
DAVE SHARPE BRAINTRUST
AARON LOPRESTI and GURU eFX COVER
KATE LEVIN PRODUCTION
NATHAN COSBY GRAY MATTER
MARK PANICCIA TEMPORAL LOBE
JOE QUESADA OVERMIND
DAN BUCKLEY COSMIC CONSCIOUSNESS
Captain America created by Joe Simon and Jack Kirby
Spotlight
MARVEL

VISIT US AT
www.abdopublishing.com

Reinforced library bound edition published in 2008 by Spotlight, a division of the ABDO Publishing Group, 8000 West 78th Street, Edina, Minnesota 55439. Spotlight produces high-quality reinforced library bound editions for schools and libraries. Published by agreement with Marvel Characters, Inc.

Library of Congress Cataloging-in-Publication Data

Parker, Jeff, 1966-
  The leader has a big head / Jeff Parker, cranium ; Manuel Garcia, hypothalamus ; Scott Koblish, corpus callosum ; Val Staples, colorhead ; Dave Sharpe, braintrust ; Aaron Lopresti and GURU eFX, cover. -- Reinforced library bound ed.
      p. cm. -- (The Avengers)
   "Marvel age"--Cover.
   Revision of issue 2 of Marvel adventures, the Avengers.
   ISBN 978-1-59961-384-0
  1. Graphic novels. I. Garcia, Manuel. II. Marvel adventures, the Avengers. 2. III. Title.

PN6728.A94P34 2008
741.5'973--dc22

                                            2007020240

All Spotlight books have reinforced library bindings and are manufactured in the United States of America.

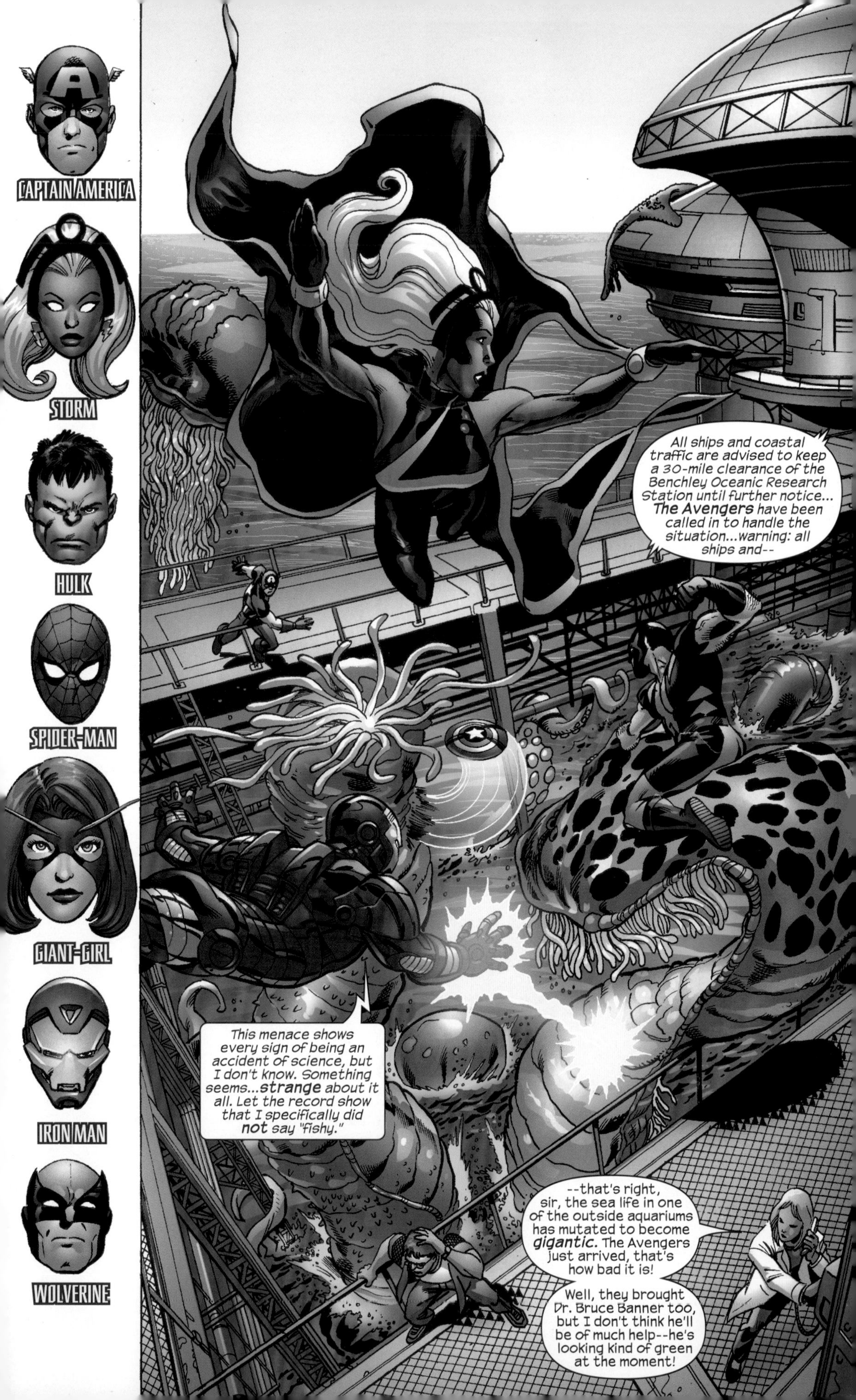
CAPTAIN AMERICA
STORM
HULK
SPIDER-MAN
GIANT-GIRL
IRON MAN
WOLVERINE
All ships and coastal traffic are advised to keep a 30-mile clearance of the Benchley Oceanic Research Station until further notice... The Avengers have been called in to handle the situation...warning: all ships and--
This menace shows every sign of being an accident of science, but I don't know. Something seems...strange about it all. Let the record show that I specifically did not say "fishy."
--that's right, sir, the sea life in one of the outside aquariums has mutated to become gigantic. The Avengers just arrived, that's how bad it is!
Well, they brought Dr. Bruce Banner too, but I don't think he'll be of much help--he's looking kind of green at the moment!

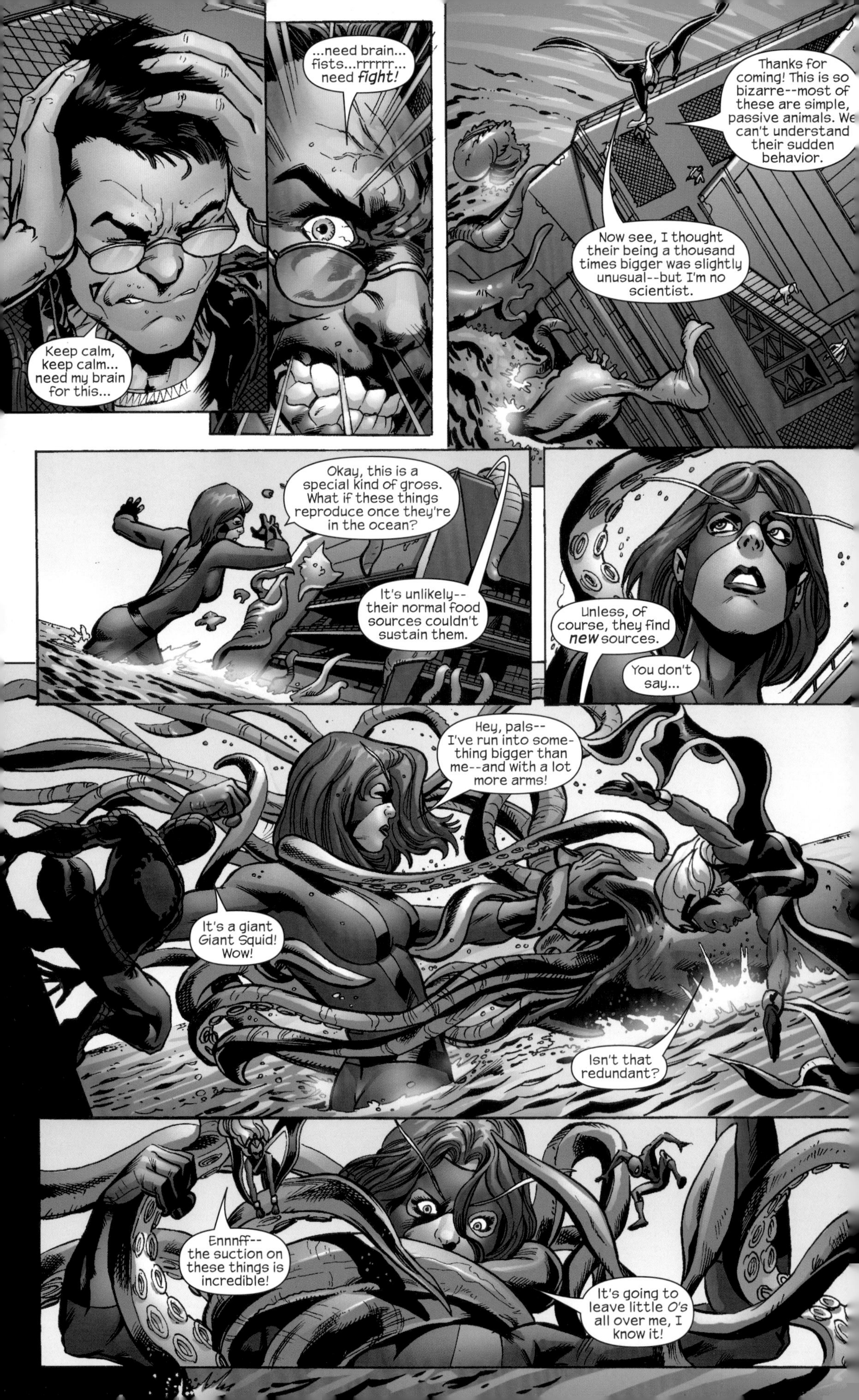
Keep calm, keep calm... need my brain for this...
...need brain... fists...rrrrrr... need *fight!*
Thanks for coming! This is so bizarre--most of these are simple, passive animals. We can't understand their sudden behavior.
Now see, I thought their being a thousand times bigger was slightly unusual--but I'm no scientist.
Okay, this is a special kind of gross. What if these things reproduce once they're in the ocean?
It's unlikely--their normal food sources couldn't sustain them.
Unless, of course, they find **new** sources.
You don't say...
Hey, pals--I've run into something bigger than me--and with a lot more arms!
It's a giant Giant Squid! Wow!
Isn't that redundant?
Ennnff--the suction on these things is incredible!
It's going to leave little *O's* all over me, I know it!

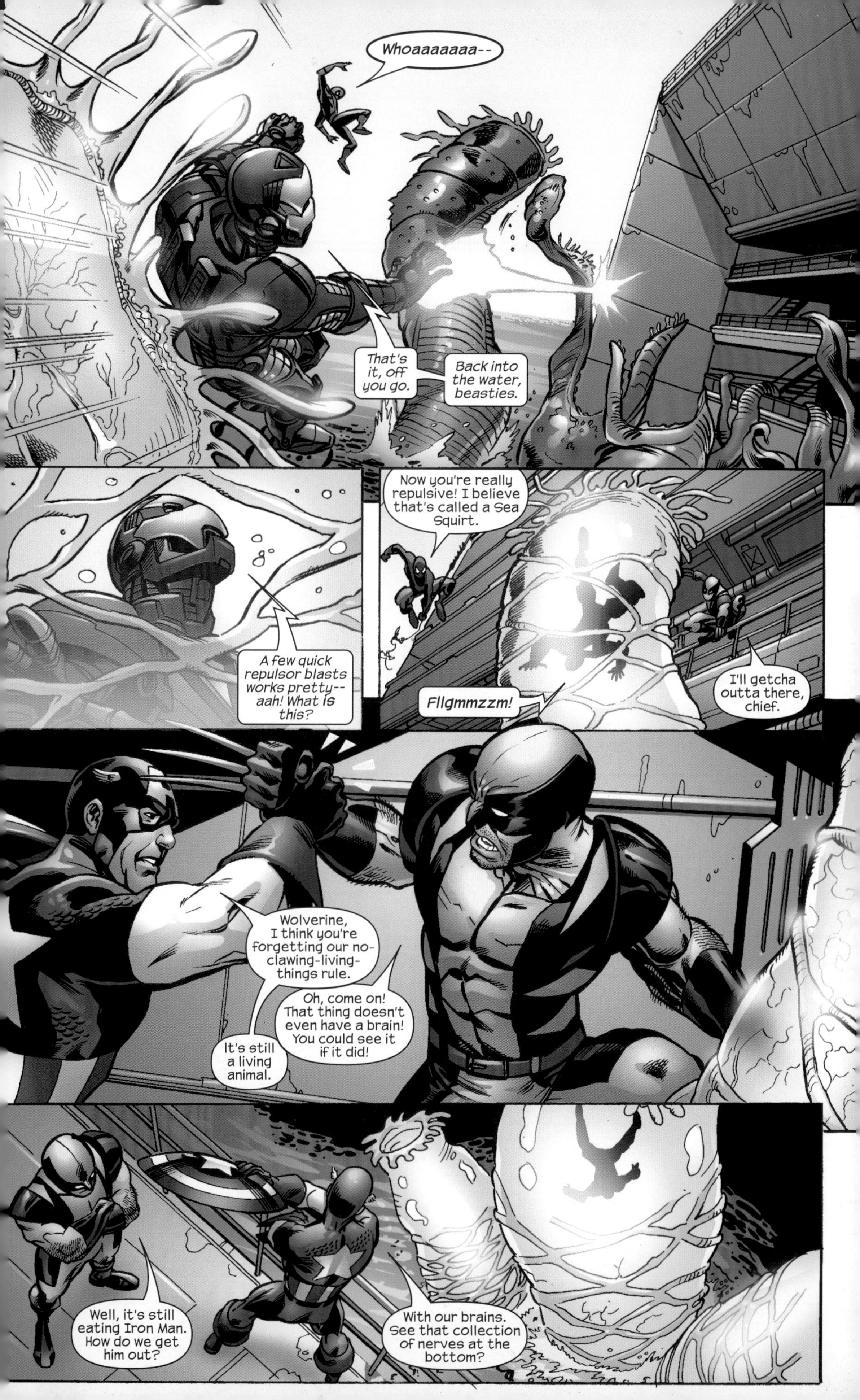
Whoaaaaaaa--
That's it, off you go.
Back into the water, beasties.
A few quick repulsor blasts works pretty-- aah! What is this?
Now you're really repulsive! I believe that's called a Sea Squirt.
Fllgmmzzm!
I'll getcha outta there, chief.
Wolverine, I think you're forgetting our no-clawing-living-things rule.
Oh, come on! That thing doesn't even have a brain! You could see it if it did!
It's still a living animal.
Well, it's still eating Iron Man. How do we get him out?
With our brains. See that collection of nerves at the bottom?

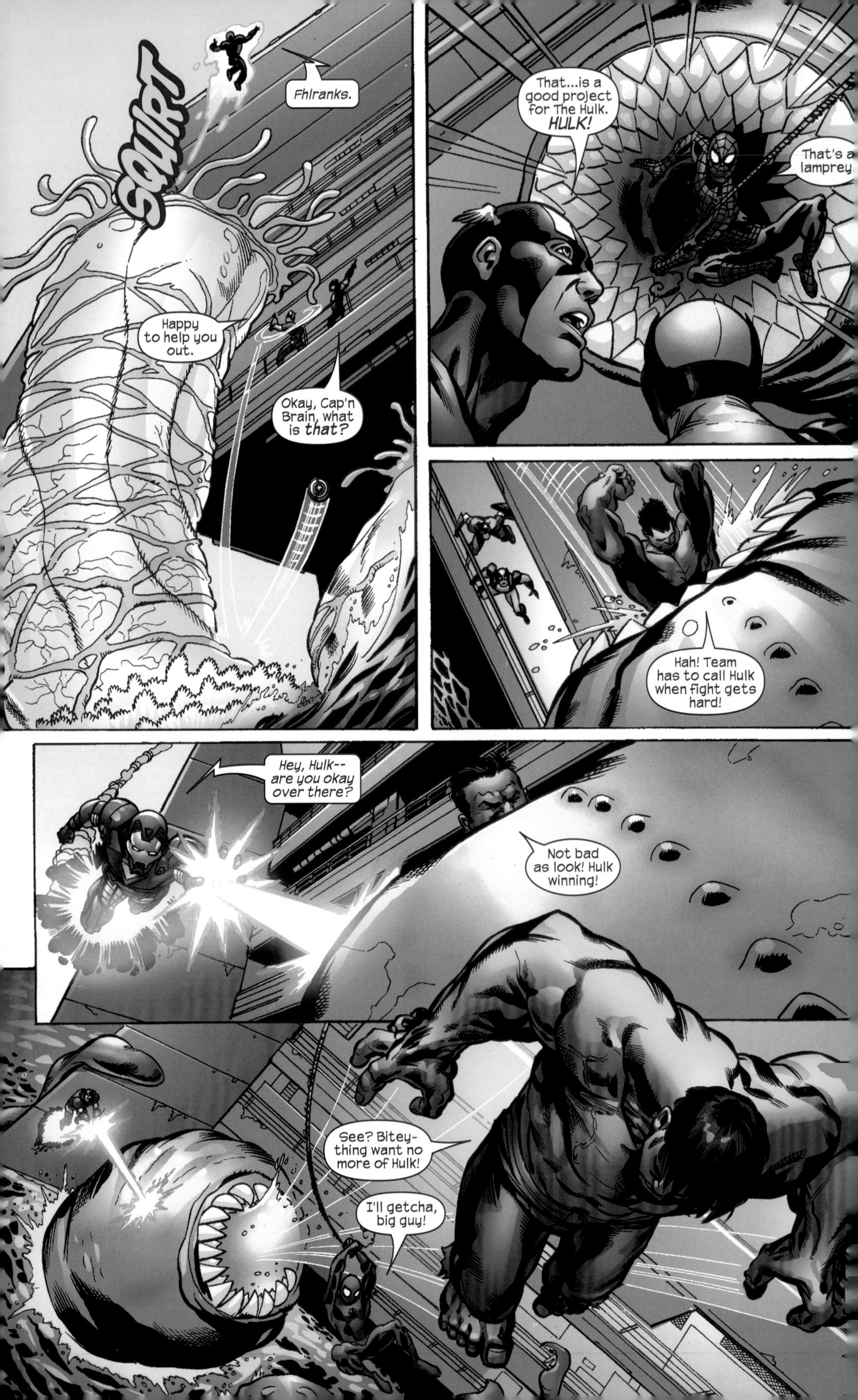
SQUIRT
Fhlranks.
Happy to help you out.
Okay, Cap'n Brain, what is that?
That...is a good project for The Hulk. HULK!
That's a lamprey
Hah! Team has to call Hulk when fight gets hard!
Hey, Hulk-- are you okay over there?
Not bad as look! Hulk winning!
See? Bitey-thing want no more of Hulk!
I'll getcha, big guy!

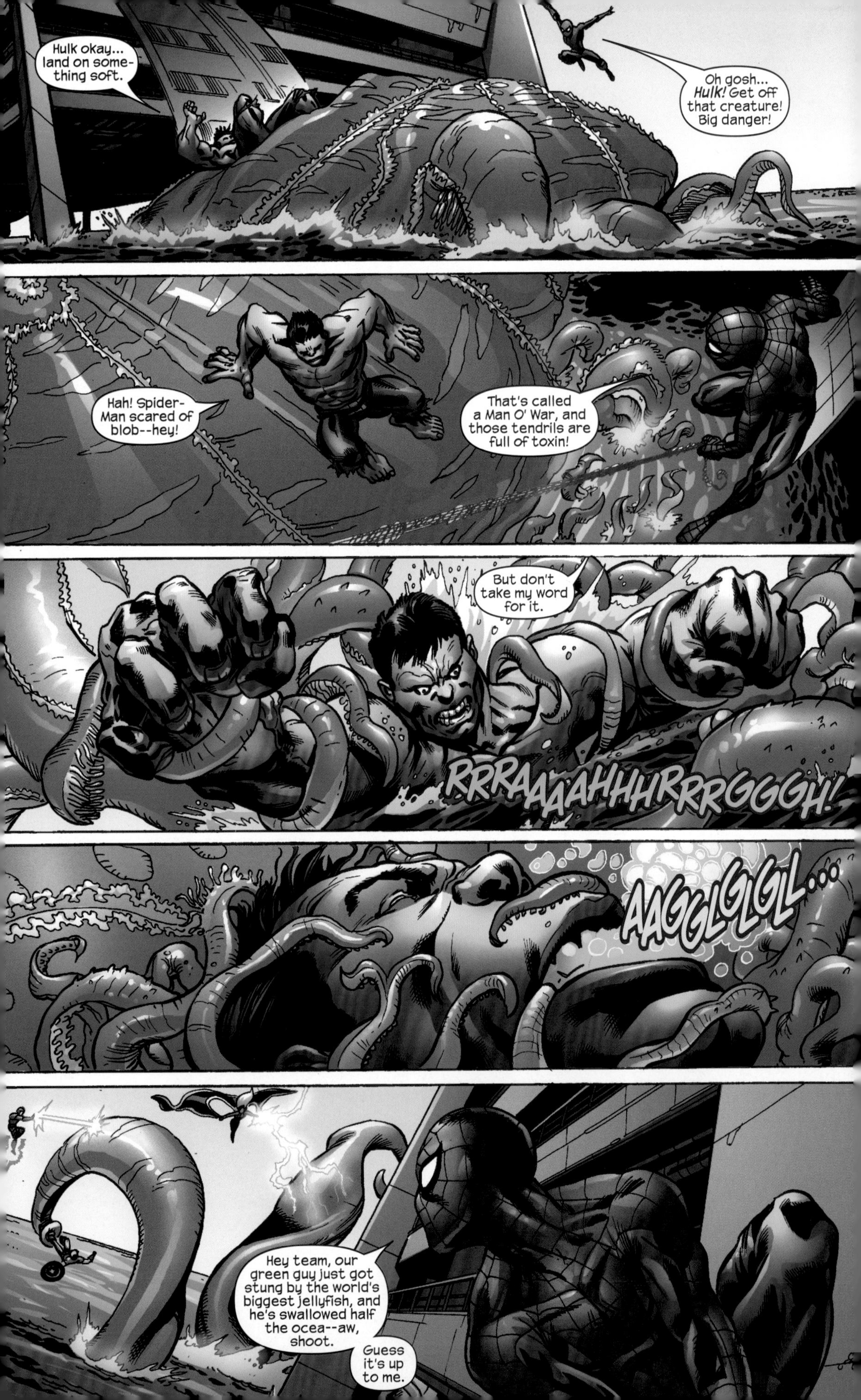
Hulk okay... land on some-thing soft.
Oh gosh... Hulk! Get off that creature! Big danger!
Hah! Spider-Man scared of blob--hey!
That's called a Man O' War, and those tendrils are full of toxin!
But don't take my word for it.
RRRAAAAHHHRRRGGGH!
AAGGLGLGLL...
Hey team, our green guy just got stung by the world's biggest jellyfish, and he's swallowed half the ocea--aw, shoot.
Guess it's up to me.

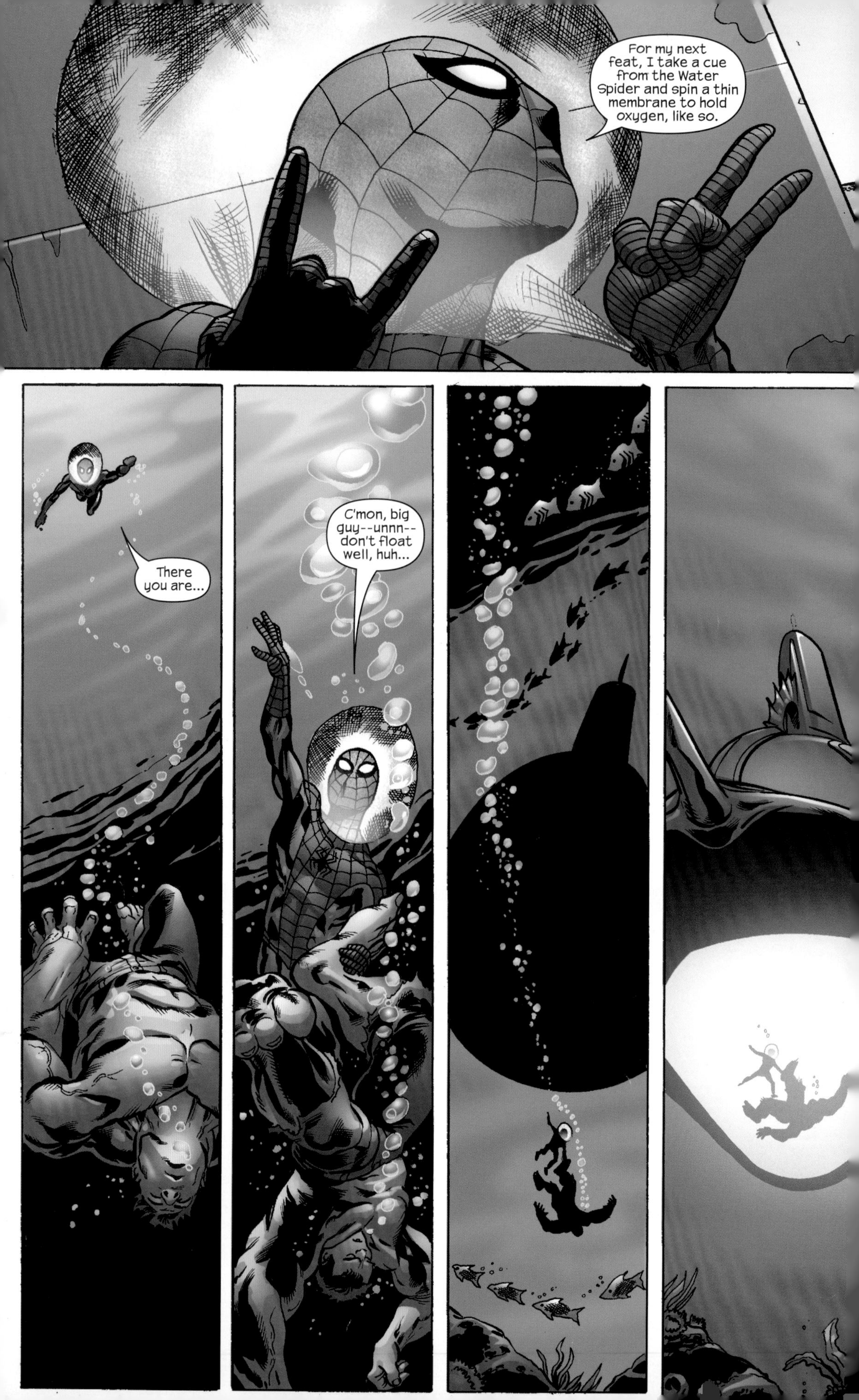

For my next feat, I take a cue from the Water Spider and spin a thin membrane to hold oxygen, like so.
There you are...
C'mon, big guy--unnn--don't float well, huh...

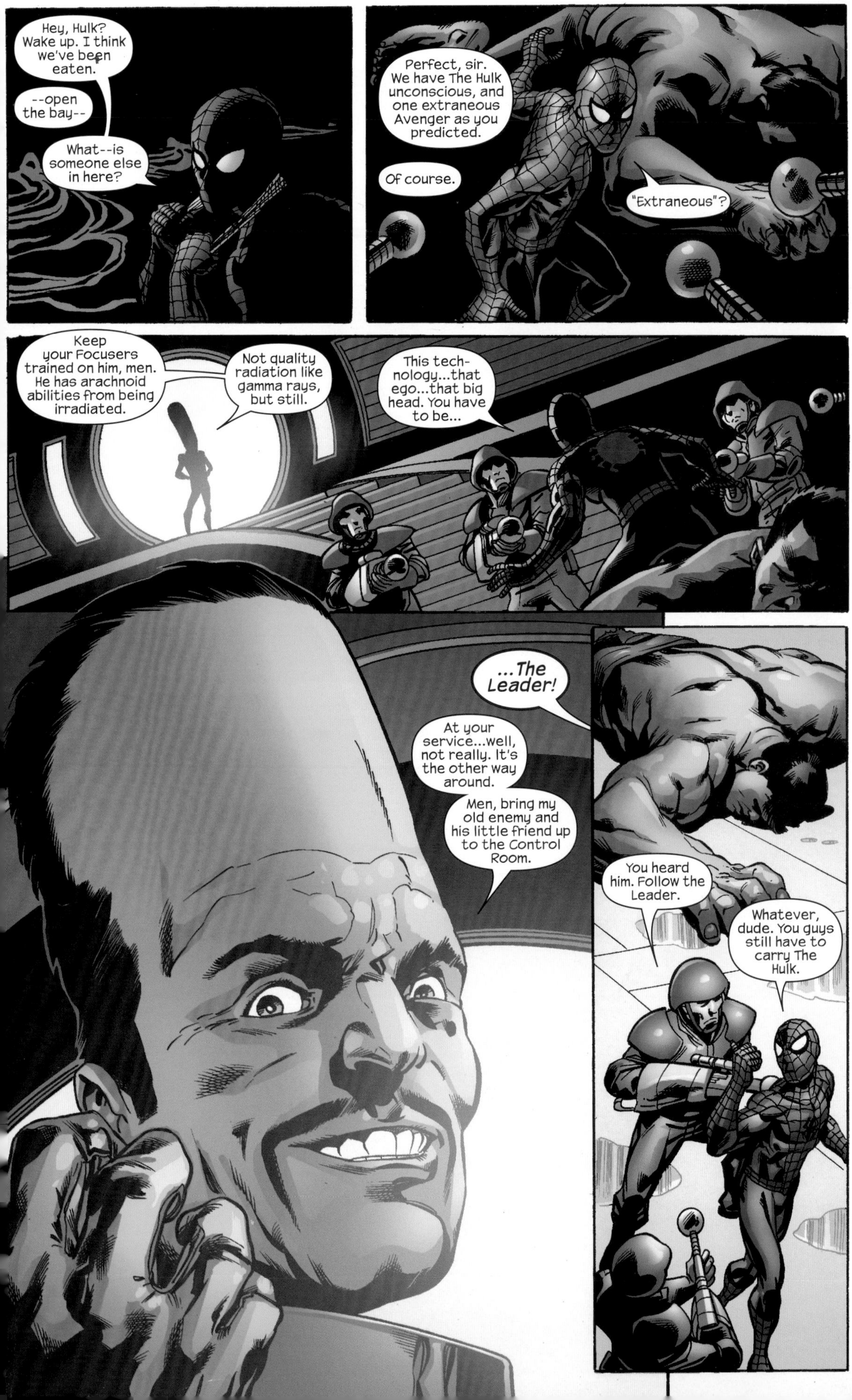

Hey, Hulk? Wake up. I think we've been eaten.
--open the bay--
What--is someone else in here?
Perfect, sir. We have The Hulk unconscious, and one extraneous Avenger as you predicted.
Of course.
"Extraneous"?
Keep your Focusers trained on him, men. He has arachnoid abilities from being irradiated.
Not quality radiation like gamma rays, but still.
This tech-nology...that ego...that big head. You have to be...
...The Leader!
At your service...well, not really. It's the other way around.
Men, bring my old enemy and his little friend up to the Control Room.
You heard him. Follow the Leader.
Whatever, dude. You guys still have to carry The Hulk.

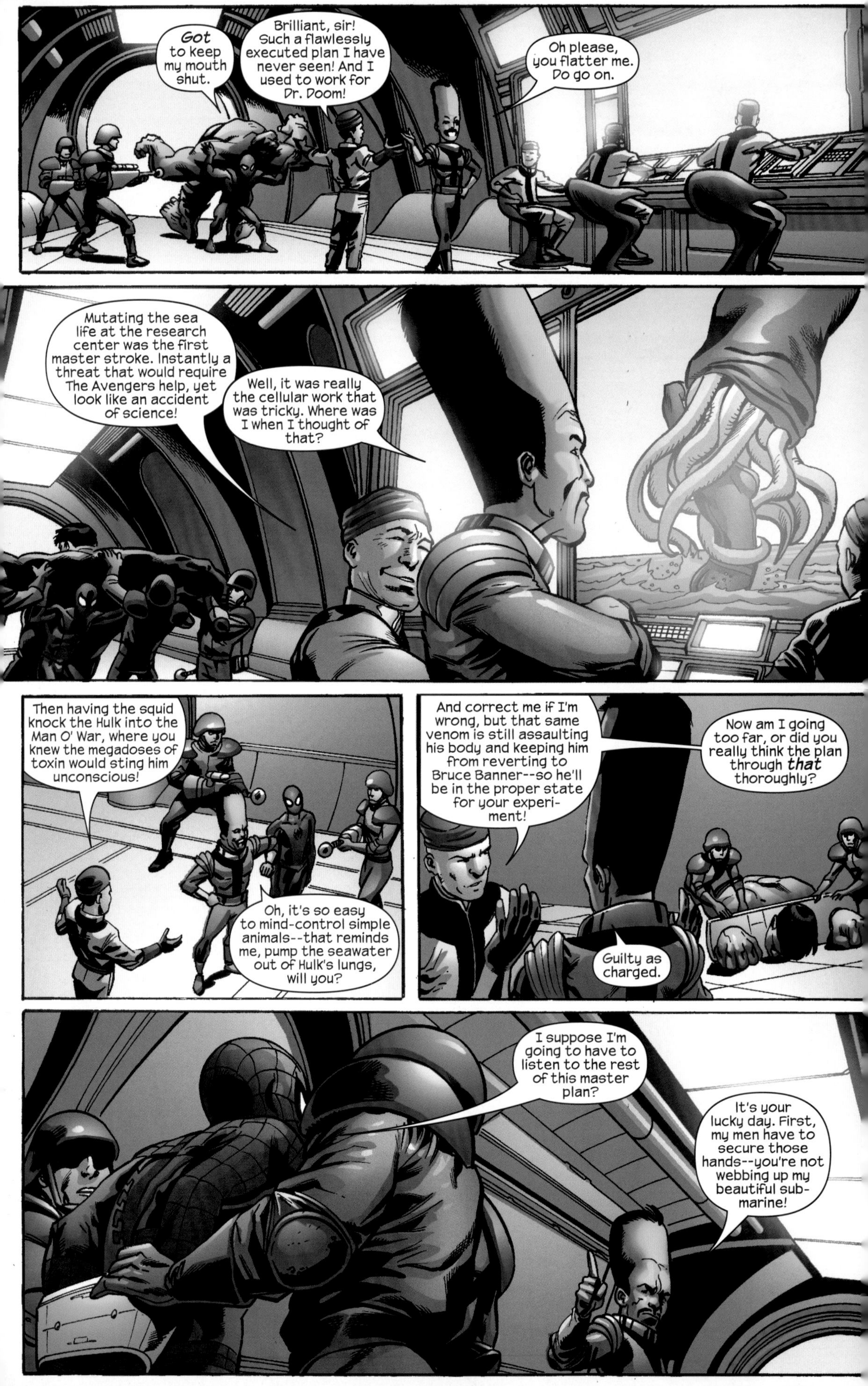
Got to keep my mouth shut.
Brilliant, sir! Such a flawlessly executed plan I have never seen! And I used to work for Dr. Doom!
Oh please, you flatter me. Do go on.
Mutating the sea life at the research center was the first master stroke. Instantly a threat that would require The Avengers help, yet look like an accident of science!
Well, it was really the cellular work that was tricky. Where was I when I thought of that?
Then having the squid knock the Hulk into the Man O' War, where you knew the megadoses of toxin would sting him unconscious!
Oh, it's so easy to mind-control simple animals--that reminds me, pump the seawater out of Hulk's lungs, will you?
And correct me if I'm wrong, but that same venom is still assaulting his body and keeping him from reverting to Bruce Banner--so he'll be in the proper state for your experi-ment!
Now am I going too far, or did you really think the plan through *that* thoroughly?
Guilty as charged.
I suppose I'm going to have to listen to the rest of this master plan?
It's your lucky day. First, my men have to secure those hands--you're not webbing up my beautiful sub-marine!

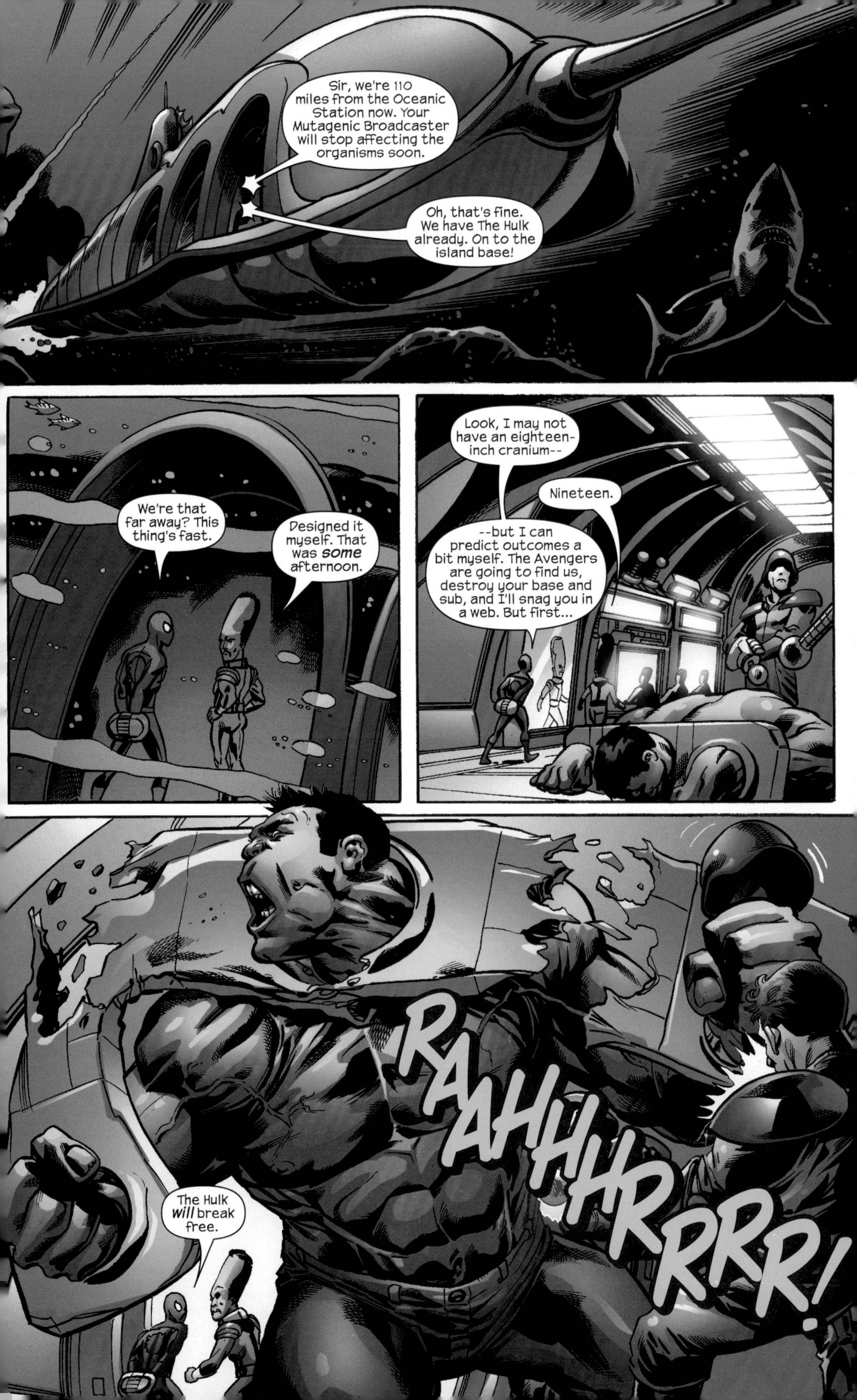
Sir, we're 110 miles from the Oceanic Station now. Your Mutagenic Broadcaster will stop affecting the organisms soon.
Oh, that's fine. We have The Hulk already. On to the island base!
We're that far away? This thing's fast.
Designed it myself. That was *some* afternoon.
Look, I may not have an eighteen-inch cranium--
Nineteen.
--but I can predict outcomes a bit myself. The Avengers are going to find us, destroy your base and sub, and I'll snag you in a web. But first...
RAAHHHRRRR!
The Hulk *will* break free.

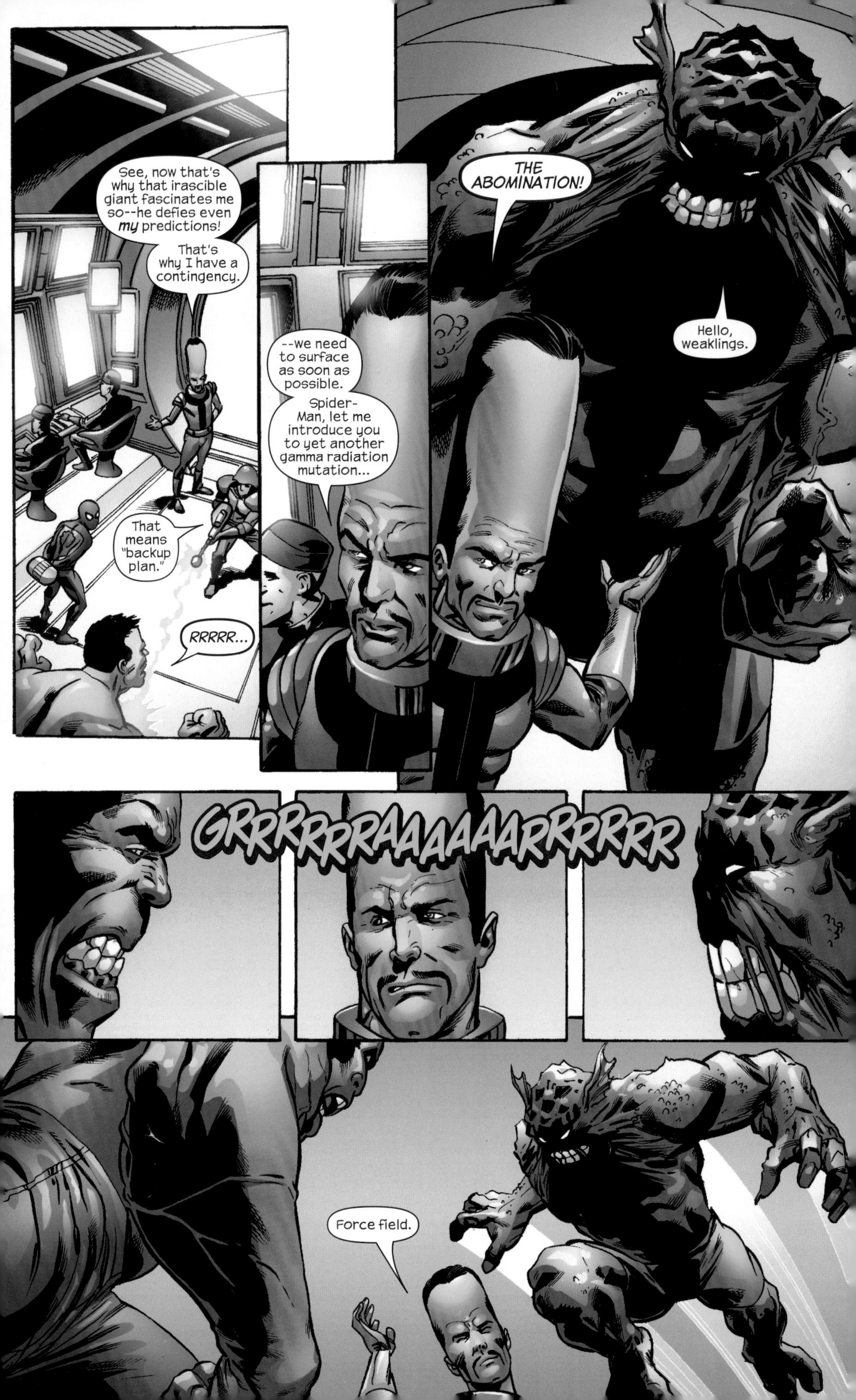
See, now that's why that irascible giant fascinates me so--he defies even *my* predictions!
That's why I have a contingency.
That means "backup plan."
RRRRR...
--we need to surface as soon as possible.
Spider-Man, let me introduce you to yet another gamma radiation mutation...
THE ABOMINATION!
Hello, weaklings.
GRRRRRRAAAAAARRRRRR
Force field.

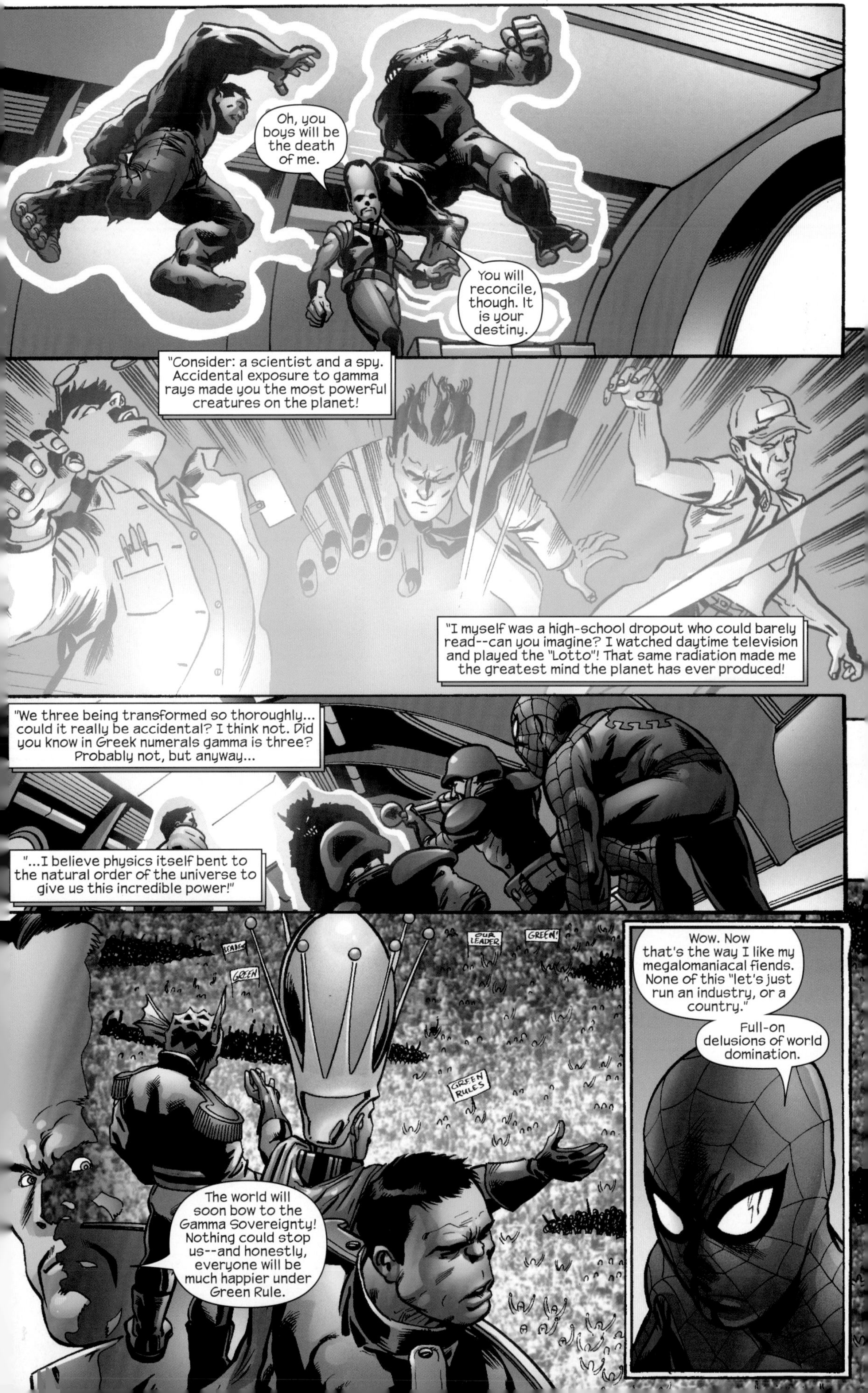
Oh, you boys will be the death of me.
You will reconcile, though. It is your destiny.
"Consider: a scientist and a spy. Accidental exposure to gamma rays made you the most powerful creatures on the planet!
"I myself was a high-school dropout who could barely read--can you imagine? I watched daytime television and played the "Lotto"! That same radiation made me the greatest mind the planet has ever produced!
"We three being transformed so thoroughly... could it really be accidental? I think not. Did you know in Greek numerals gamma is three? Probably not, but anyway...
"...I believe physics itself bent to the natural order of the universe to give us this incredible power!"
OUR LEADER
GREEN!
GREEN
GREEN RULES
The world will soon bow to the Gamma Sovereignty! Nothing could stop us--and honestly, everyone will be much happier under Green Rule.
Wow. Now that's the way I like my megalomaniacal fiends. None of this "let's just run an industry, or a country."
Full-on delusions of world domination.

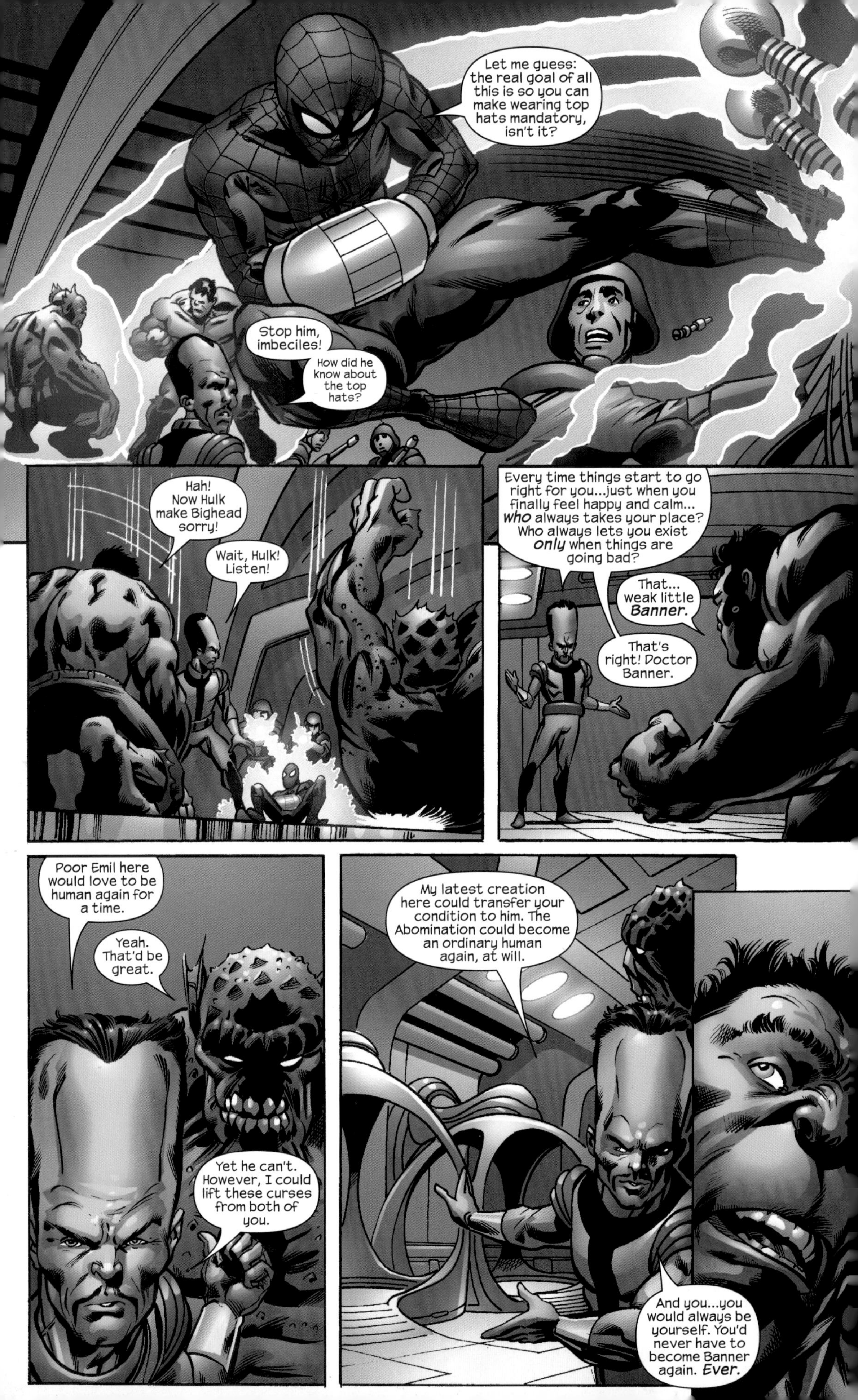
Let me guess: the real goal of all this is so you can make wearing top hats mandatory, isn't it?
Stop him, imbeciles!
How did he know about the top hats?
Hah! Now Hulk make Bighead sorry!
Wait, Hulk! Listen!
Every time things start to go right for you...just when you finally feel happy and calm... *who* always takes your place? Who always lets you exist *only* when things are going bad?
That... weak little *Banner.*
That's right! Doctor Banner.
Poor Emil here would love to be human again for a time.
Yeah. That'd be great.
Yet he can't. However, I could lift these curses from both of you.
My latest creation here could transfer your condition to him. The Abomination could become an ordinary human again, at will.
And you...you would always be yourself. You'd never have to become Banner again. *Ever.*

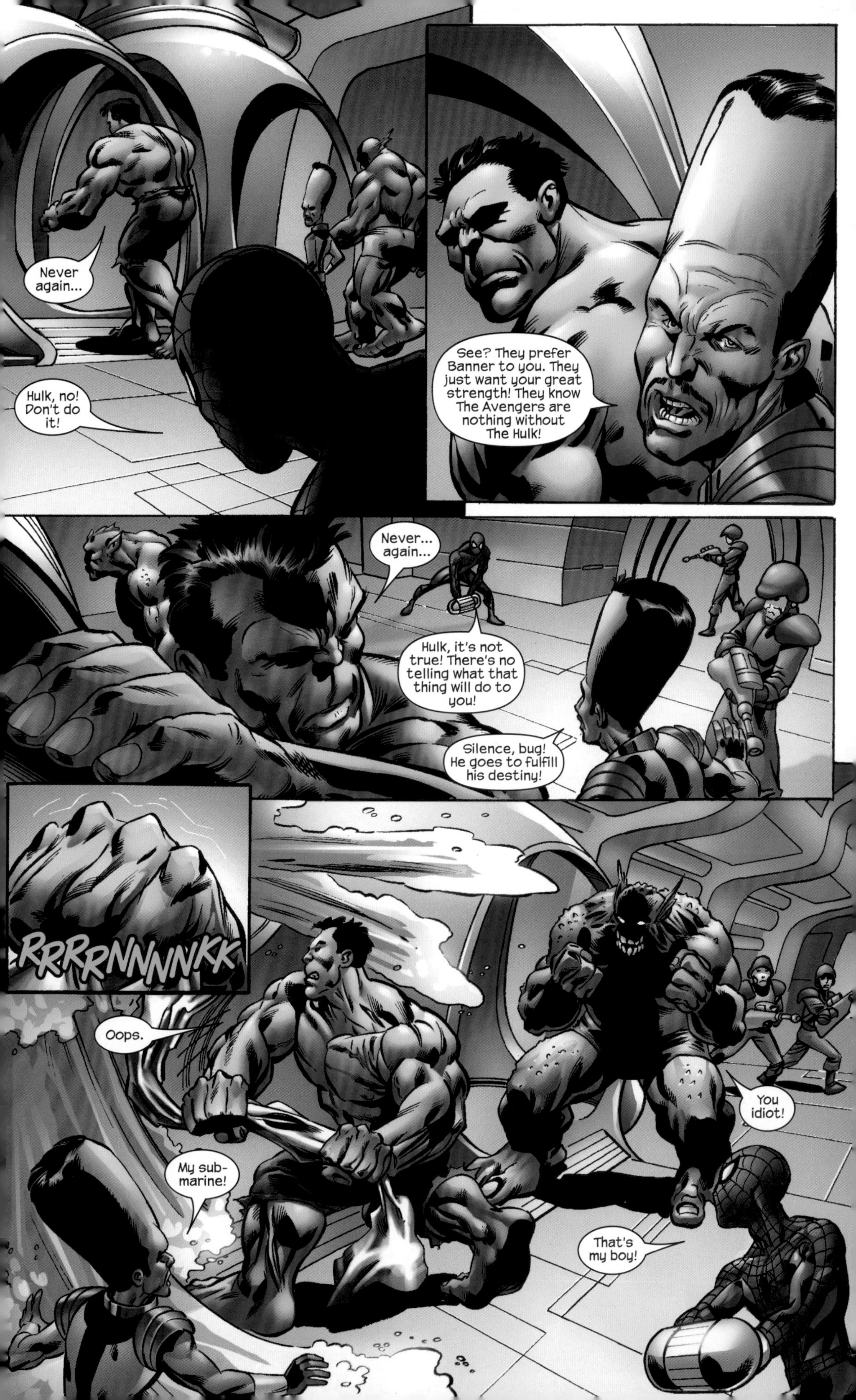
Never again...
Hulk, no! Don't do it!
See? They prefer Banner to you. They just want your great strength! They know The Avengers are nothing without The Hulk!
Never... again...
Hulk, it's not true! There's no telling what that thing will do to you!
Silence, bug! He goes to fulfill his destiny!
RRRRNNNNNKK
Oops.
My sub-marine!
You idiot!
That's my boy!

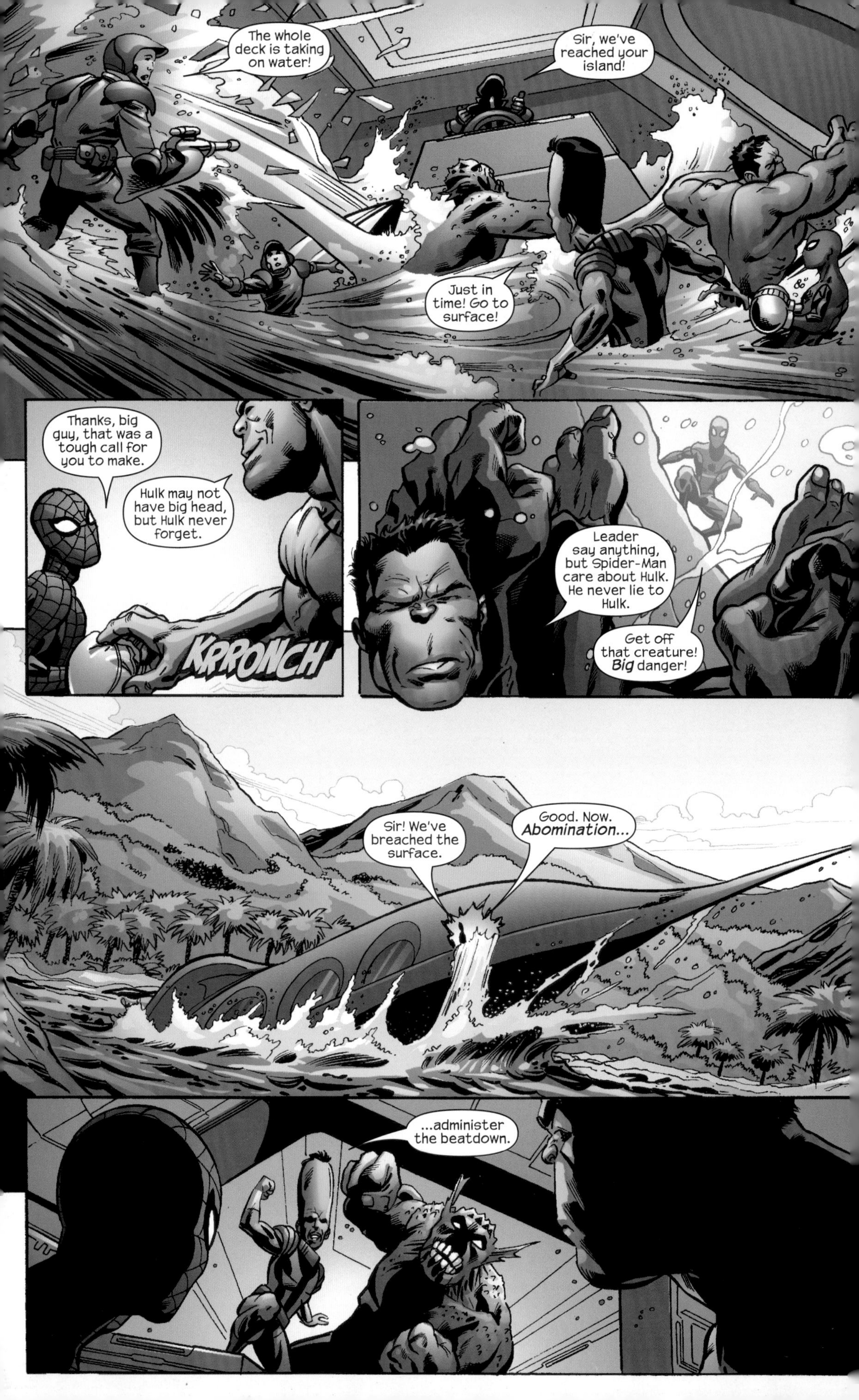
The whole deck is taking on water!
Sir, we've reached your island!
Just in time! Go to surface!
Thanks, big guy, that was a tough call for you to make.
Hulk may not have big head, but Hulk never forget.
KRRONCH
Leader say anything, but Spider-Man care about Hulk. He never lie to Hulk.
Get off that creature! Big danger!
Sir! We've breached the surface.
Good. Now. Abomination...
...administer the beatdown.

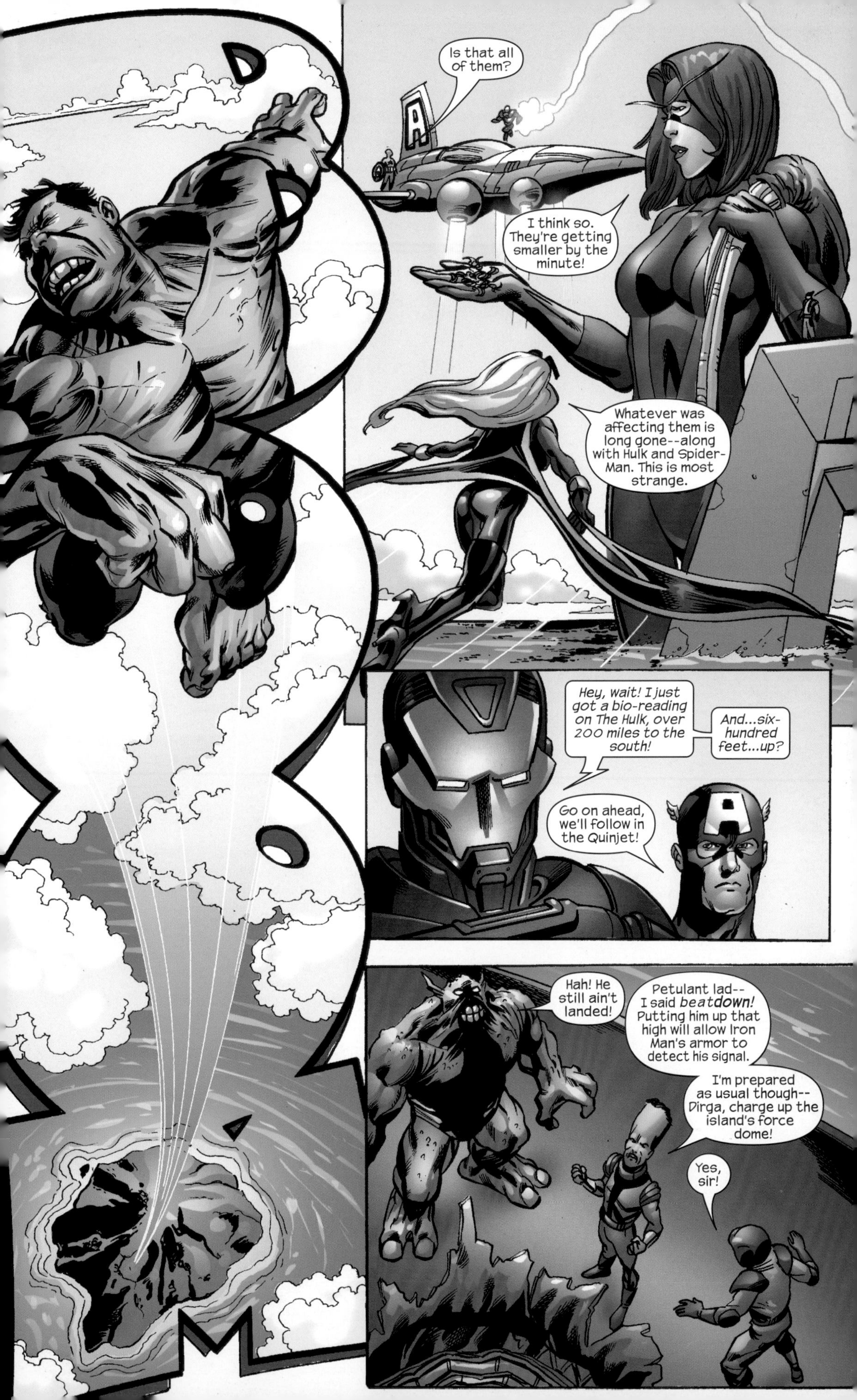
Is that all of them?
I think so. They're getting smaller by the minute!
Whatever was affecting them is long gone--along with Hulk and Spider-Man. This is most strange.
Hey, wait! I just got a bio-reading on The Hulk, over 200 miles to the south!
And...six-hundred feet...up?
Go on ahead, we'll follow in the Quinjet!
Hah! He still ain't landed!
Petulant lad--I said beatdown! Putting him up that high will allow Iron Man's armor to detect his signal.
I'm prepared as usual though--Dirga, charge up the island's force dome!
Yes, sir!

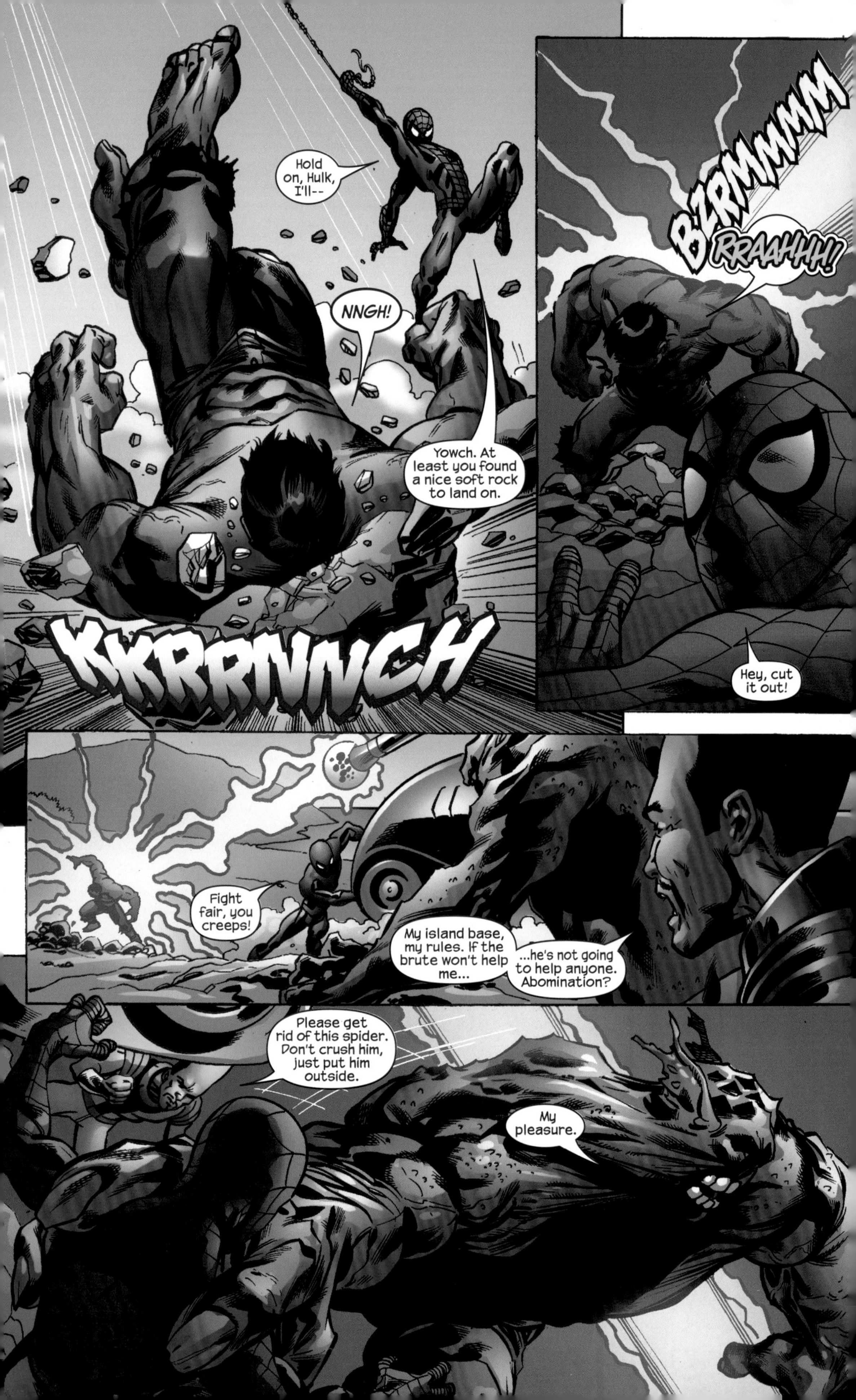

Hold on, Hulk, I'll--
NNGH!
Yowch. At least you found a nice soft rock to land on.
KKRRNNCH
BZRMMMM
RRAAHHH!
Hey, cut it out!
Fight fair, you creeps!
My island base, my rules. If the brute won't help me...
...he's not going to help anyone. Abomination?
Please get rid of this spider. Don't crush him, just put him outside.
My pleasure.

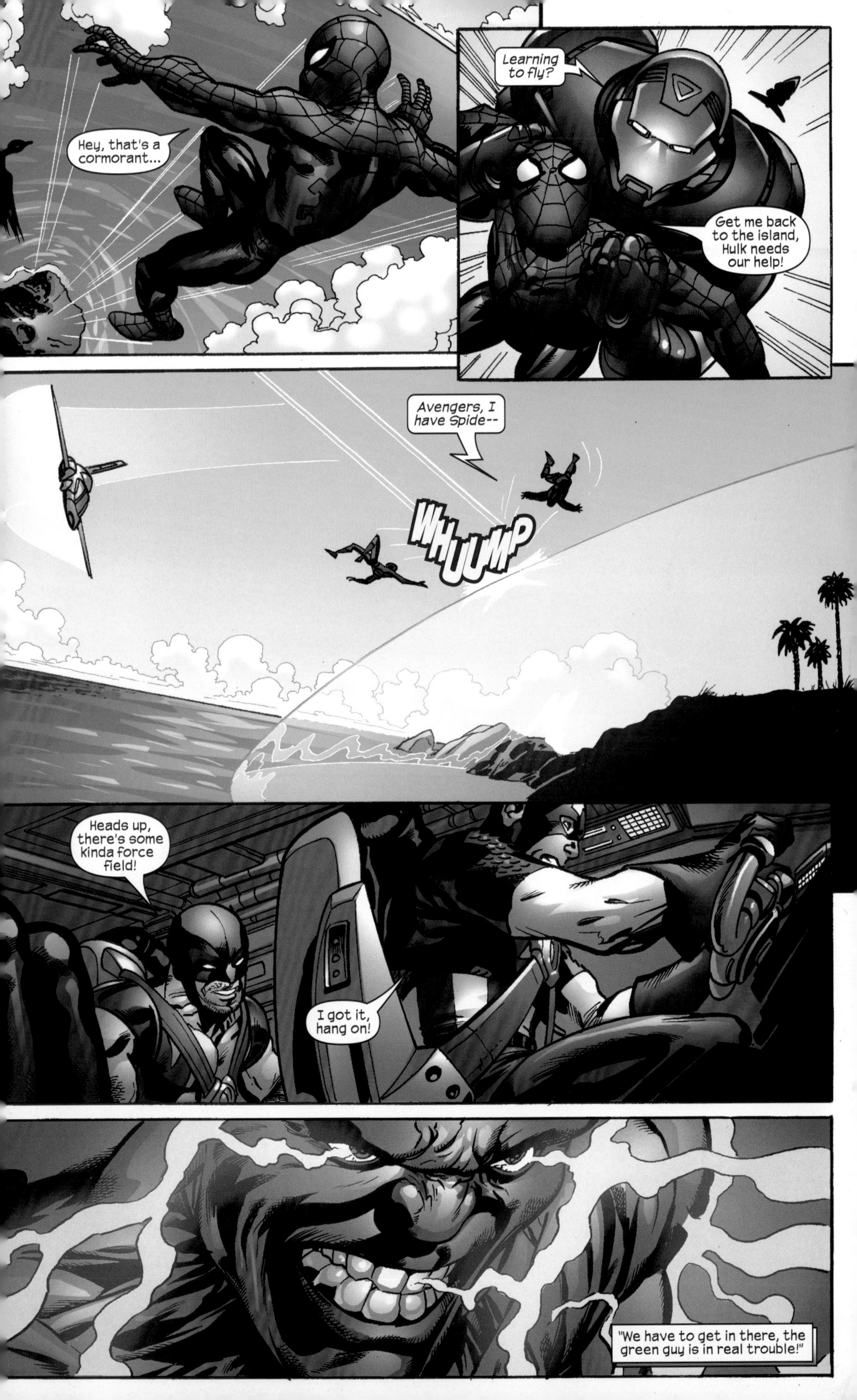
Hey, that's a cormorant...
Learning to fly?
Get me back to the island, Hulk needs our help!
Avengers, I have Spide--
WHUUMP
Heads up, there's some kinda force field!
I got it, hang on!
"We have to get in there, the green guy is in real trouble!"

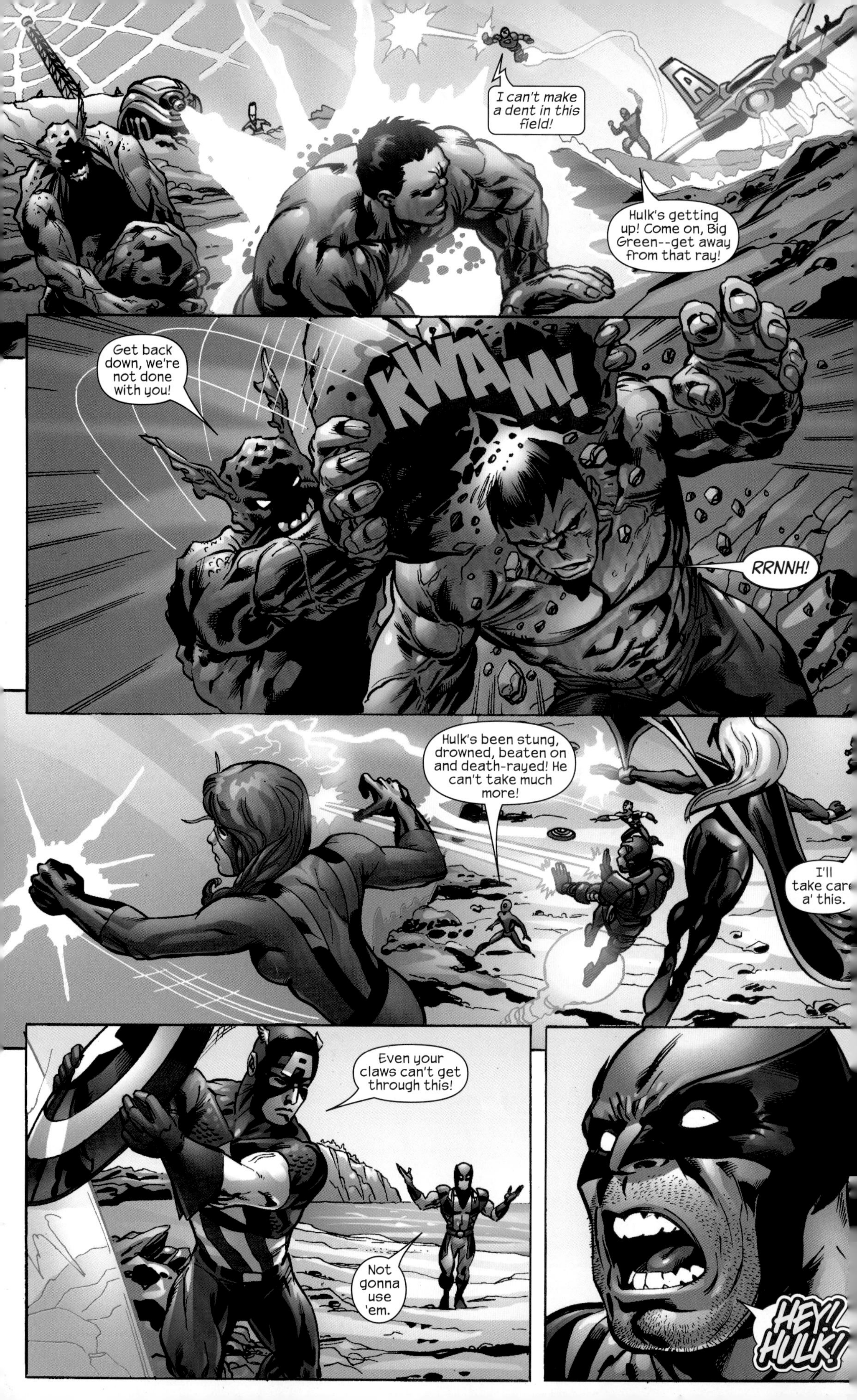
I can't make a dent in this field!
Hulk's getting up! Come on, Big Green--get away from that ray!
Get back down, we're not done with you!
KWAM!
RRNNH!
Hulk's been stung, drowned, beaten on and death-rayed! He can't take much more!
I'll take care a' this.
Even your claws can't get through this!
Not gonna use 'em.
HEY! HULK!

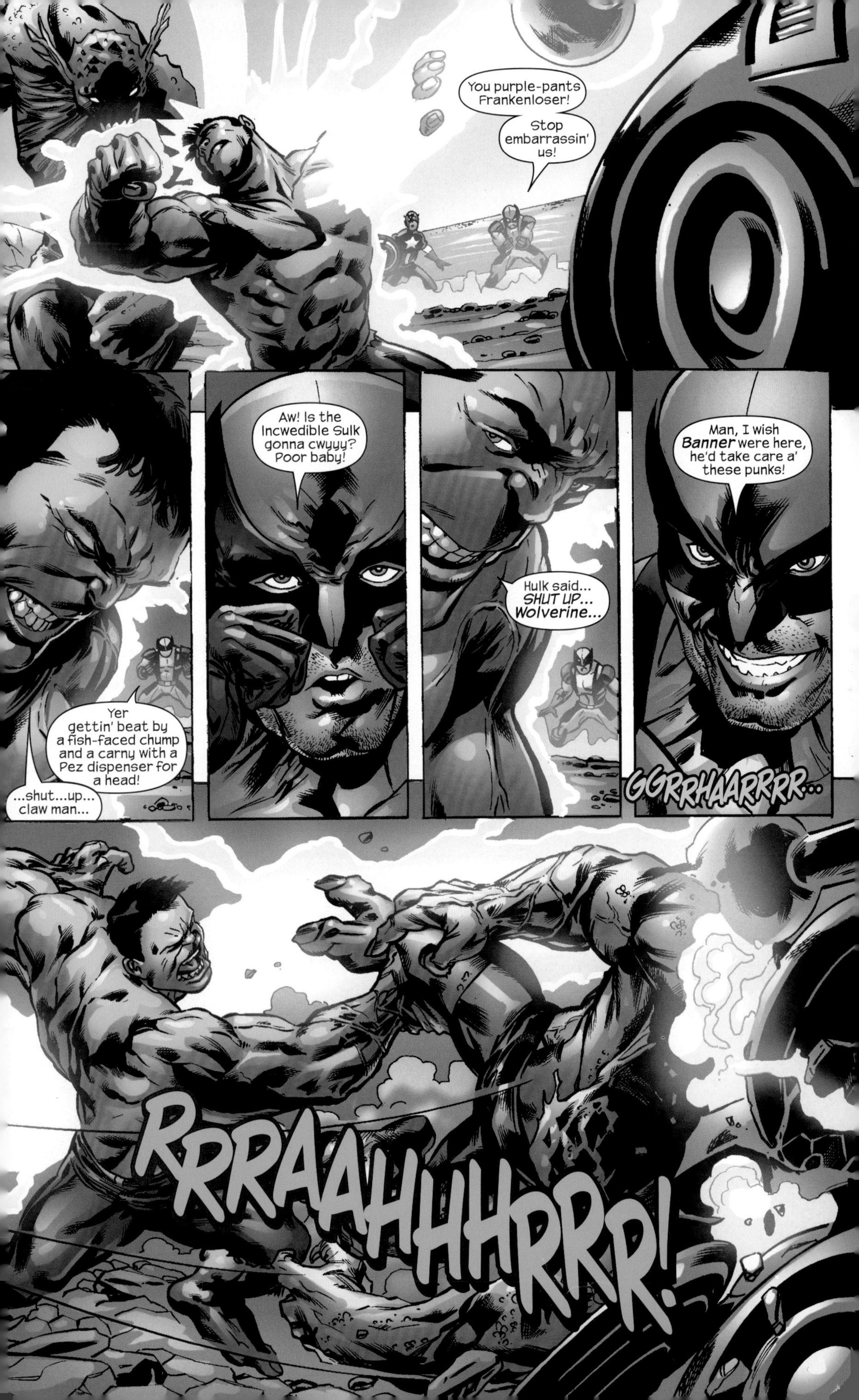
You purple-pants Frankenloser!
Stop embarrassin' us!
Yer gettin' beat by a fish-faced chump and a carny with a Pez dispenser for a head!
...shut...up... claw man...
Aw! Is the Incwedible Sulk gonna cwyyy? Poor baby!
Hulk said... SHUT UP... Wolverine...
Man, I wish Banner were here, he'd take care a' these punks!
GGRRHAARRRR...
RRRAAHHHRRR!

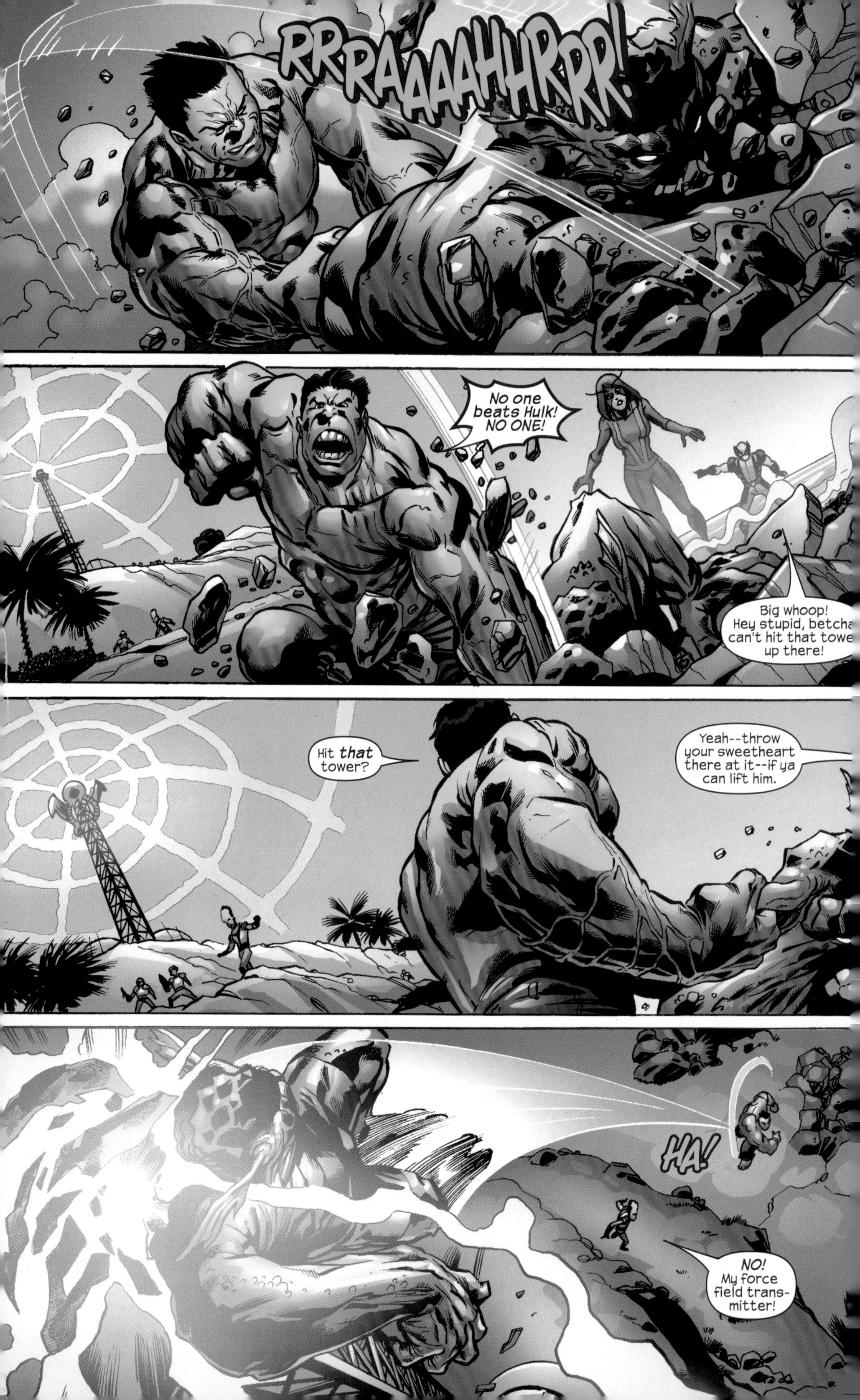
RRRAAAAHHRRR!
No one beats Hulk! NO ONE!
Big whoop! Hey stupid, betcha can't hit that towe up there!
Hit *that* tower?
Yeah--throw your sweetheart there at it--if ya can lift him.
HA!
NO! My force field trans-mitter!

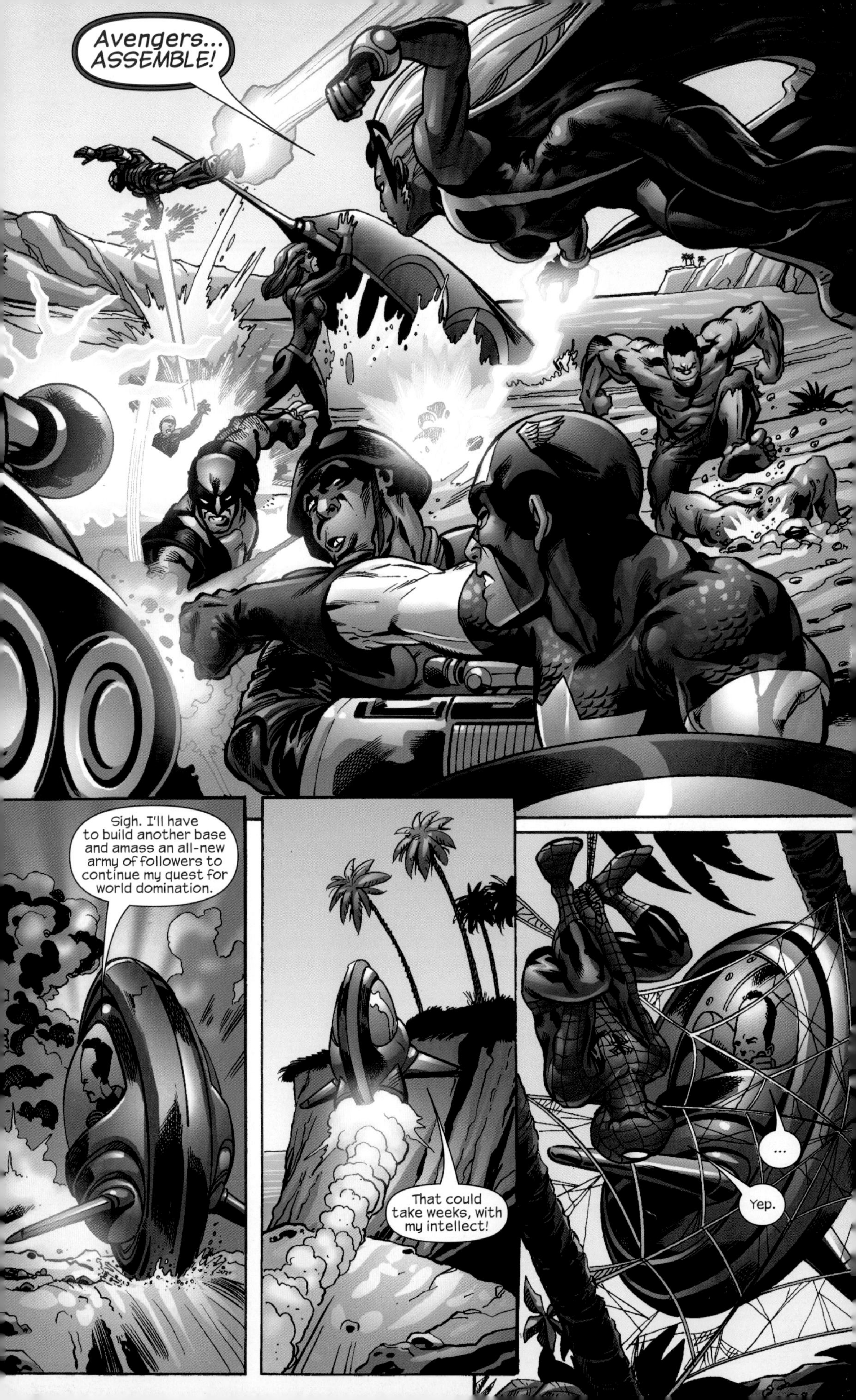
Avengers... ASSEMBLE!
Sigh. I'll have to build another base and amass an all-new army of followers to continue my quest for world domination.
That could take weeks, with my intellect!
...
Yep.

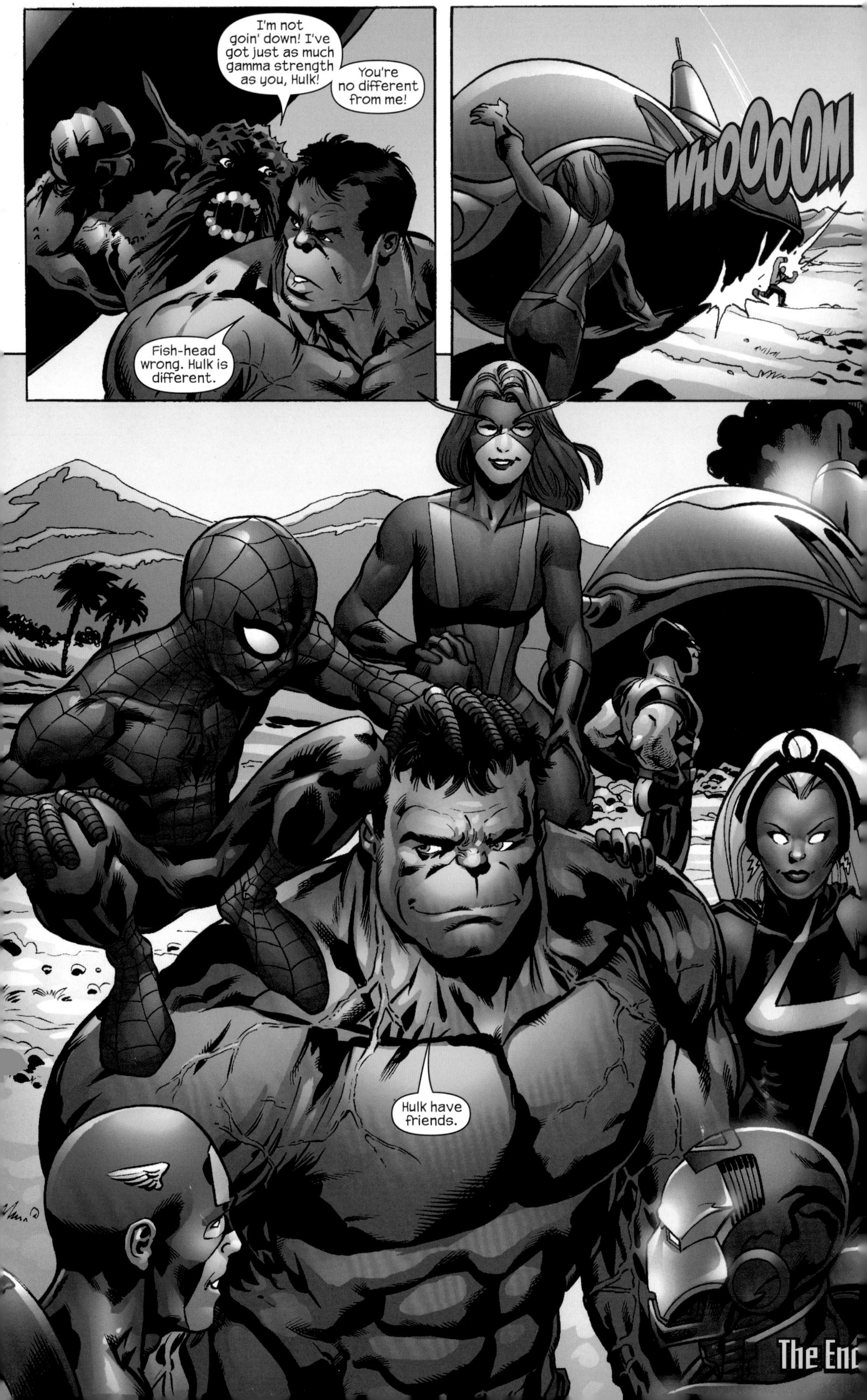
I'm not goin' down! I've got just as much gamma strength as you, Hulk!
You're no different from me!
Fish-head wrong. Hulk is different.
WHOOOOOM
Hulk have friends.